Edward and the Eureka Lucky Wish Company

To Aberash and Yalfal, who know how to fly — B.T.

For my family — P.S.

Kids Can Press acknowledges the financial support of
the Government of Ontario, through the Ontario Media
Development Corporation's Ontario Book Initiative; the
Ontario Arts Council; the Canada Council for the Arts; and
the Government of Canada, through the BPIDP, for our
publishing activity.

Published in Canada by
Kids Can Press Ltd.
29 Birch Avenue
Toronto, ON M4V 1E2

Published in the U.S. by
Kids Can Press Ltd.
2250 Military Road
Tonawanda, NY 14150

www.kidscanpress.com

The artwork in this book was rendered in pencil, India ink
and Adobe Photoshop.
The text is set in McKracken.

Edited by Yvette Ghione
Designed by Julia Naimska and Kathleen Gray
Printed and bound in China

This book is smyth sewn casebound.

CM 09 0 9 8 7 6 5 4 3 2 1

Library and Archives Canada Cataloguing in Publication

Todd, Barbara, 1961-
     Edward and the Eureka Lucky Wish Company /
Barbara Todd ; illustrated by Patricia Storms.

Interest age level: For ages 4-7.
ISBN 978-1-55453-264-3

I. Storms, Patricia II. Title.

PS8589.059E49 2009   jC813'.6   C2008-903322-1

Kids Can Press is a *Corus*™ Entertainment company

Edward and the Eureka Lucky Wish Company

Written by **Barbara Todd**

Illustrated by **Patricia Storms**

KIDS CAN PRESS

Edward adjusted the splurchler on his flying machine, the Sky-Hopper 2000. He checked the figgler and gave the turbo-twirler a spin. "Ready for takeoff!"

CRUNNCH!

"Aww, this thing's never going to fly!" grumped Edward.
"Why don't you go to the park?" suggested his mother. She gave him some money for a hot dog.
"The park?" moaned Edward. "Ho hum."

But Edward went.

When he got there, Edward spied a booth next to the hot dog man's cart.

"Wishes?" he said. "Eureka!"

"Be careful," said the salesman. "A lot can happen with three wishes." He handed Edward a coupon, then folded up the booth, swirled his cloak around him and disappeared.

EUREKA LUCKY WISH COMPANY
Buy Two. Get One Free.

"Wow!" whispered Edward.
He read the coupon:

★ Good for ★
THREE WISHES

"Here goes." Edward closed his eyes.
"I wish my Sky-Hopper 2000 would fly."

Edward heard a boing!

And a sproing!

Then

Z-Z-ZOOOM!

The Sky-Hopper 2000 took off.
"Hey!" cried Edward. "What about me?"

When Edward got home, there was the Sky-Hopper 2000.
"I can't believe I wasted a perfectly good wish," he grumbled.
His mother called, "Edward, time to clean your room."
"Aww," said Edward. "I wish I didn't have to clean my room."

Upstairs, he found a
sign on his bedroom door.
"Who put that there?"
Edward opened the door.

"Yikes!" yelped Edward. A slurping, burping Bog Bubbler was gobbling up everything! "Now I *can't* clean my room. There's nothing left!" He scribbled a new sign.

BEWARE
OF
MONSTER

"I'll have to be more careful with my last wish."

"Edward, time for supper. It's Brussels Sprouts Surprise!" called his mother.

"Oh, no!" cried Edward. "Brussels sprouts? I wish I — *oomph!*" Edward stopped just in time. "Arghhh! I could rid the world of brussels sprouts forever! But can I really waste my last wish on *vegetables?!* "

Before Edward could decide, the Bog Bubbler glopped down the stairs and oozed under the table.

Edward hurried after him.

SLURRRP!

Surprise! Bog Bubblers love brussels sprouts!
Edward was thrilled.

Edward's mother was delighted. "More, son?"

"More?" squeaked Edward. Now what?

While his mother cleared the dishes, Edward tiptoed upstairs, leaving a tantalizing trail of brussels sprouts behind him.

The Bog Bubbler ate up every last bit.

Quickly, Edward shut his door on the Bog Bubbler. "Phew! That was close."

"Edward, time for your bath," called his mother.

"Aww," he muttered. "I wish I didn't have to take a bath." Edward gasped. "Holy macaroni! My *last* wish!"

Edward raced to the bathroom. The bathtub was gone. "Now I *can't* take a bath. Somebody's already taken it!"

Edward heard a commotion and went
to the window. "That's *my* bathtub!"
There was Quackie, the wind-up
duck, and Norton, his plastic shark. But
now polar bears were sitting in his tub.
Edward ran outside.

A penguin waved a flag, "On your mark. Get set. Go!" Bathtubs splished across the lawn. They splashed through the garden.

"Come back!" wailed Edward. But he had more important things to worry about. The Bog Bubbler was bubbling out of Edward's bedroom window.

"Uh-oh." Edward gulped. "Hungry again?"

The monster blobbed toward him and slurped.

"Yikes! Wait for me!" Edward blurted, hurtling into the tub as the polar bears sailed past.

"Edward!" It was his mother.

"I can explain!" he began, but his mother didn't look the least bit worried. Edward turned around.

No bathtubs. No monsters. No puddles, polar bears or penguins.

"It's after eight o'clock," said his mother. "Time to get ready for bed."

"Bed? But I don't get it!" Edward dashed upstairs to check his bedroom.

"Messy, just like always." He checked the bathtub. "Right where it's supposed to be. There must be something wrong with this coupon."

Edward held his magnifying glass over the fine print and read, "'*Expires Saturday. Eight o'clock. Dial 123-WISH.*' Hey, my wishes expired! And I never even got to fly." He dialed the number.

"Eureka Lucky Wish Company, Walter speaking."

"My wishes disappeared," explained Edward. "And there was something strange about them."

"You must have gotten the Strange and Unusual Wish coupon. Why not try one of our Ordinary and Everyday Wishes?"

"Ordinary wishes?" said Edward. "Ho hum."

"We've also got High Up and Down Wishes; Inside and Out Wishes; Nearly Unsqueezable, Almost Unseeable, Slightly Invisible Wishes and —" Walter paused to catch his breath.

"I wish there weren't so many," interrupted Edward.

"Watch what you're wishing!" warned Walter. "How about our Humdinger Lucky Wish Special?"

"What's that?"

"Something you've always dreamed of," Walter answered. "But it's got to be a real humdinger."

"That's easy," Edward said. "I wish I could fly."

"No problem," said Walter.

"But wait!" added Edward. "I need my Sky-Hopper 2000."

"Okey-dokey," said Walter.

Edward raced outside.

"Ready for takeoff!" he called.

Edward felt a slight breeze. Two pelicans flapped their wings as they landed beside him.

"Welcome aboard," squawked the first bird.

"Never flown before?" asked the second bird, scooping Edward up. "Nothing to be afraid of."

"We'll be serving lunch in a few minutes," announced the first bird. He was the pilot.

"Ish fish," mumbled the second bird.

"Ooh!" said the pilot. "Is this a Sky-Hopper 2000?"

"Yup," said Edward. "I made it myself. But it's not quite right yet."

"Maybe if you switched the splurchler with the figgler?"

"Good idea," agreed Edward, adjusting the flying machine.

"Can I take it for a spin?" asked the pilot.

"Sure," said Edward. He didn't mind so much. After all, he'd never traveled by pelican before, either.

"Ready for takeoff?" the pilot asked.

"Ready," said Edward.

First they flew over the park.
Then they stopped for a hot dog.
"Your turn," said the pilot.

Edward climbed aboard the Sky-Hopper 2000. He gave the turbo-twirler a spin.

"Nice job," said the pilot. "See you at the park?"

"See you at the park," said Edward.

"Ready for takeoff?" the pilot asked.

"Ready," said Edward.

Then Edward pedaled down the sidewalk and flew all the way home.